Bing

Bed Time

by Ted Dewan

David Fickling Books

OXFORD · NEW YORK

**Round the corner,
Not far away,
Bing has had a lovely day.**

Hello
Bing.

Hello
Flop.

Do you know
what time
it is?

It's Bed Time.

Ok Bing. Come on.

It's **Bed Time.**

Bing Bunny!

Bed Time!

Time to sit
on the potty
and try.

Nothing? OK.
Try again later.

Then
brushy
brush
teeth

and
spit out
the
yuck –

ptoo!

Now fling off your clothes

and let's play in the bath –
whee!

Quick!

Wrap up in a
cosy warm towel.

OK, Bing, let's calm down, and put on your pyjamas.

That's good, Bing!
Now let's choose
a story

and cuddle up
with Flop.

Is he under the covers?

Nope.

Is he playing hide and seek?

Nope.

Is he outside alone in the dark?

Nope.

Poor Flop.
He's lost.

Wait a minute...what's that under the bed?

Can't have Bed Time without Flop!

Big lights off.
Night light
on.

Goodnight Flop.
Goodnight Bing.

Bing?

Where's
Bing?

There you are.
You went all
by yourself!

Good for you,
Bing Bunny!

That's
better.

Bed
Time.

It's a
Bing Thing.